powerful man in the universe and the protector of Castle Grayskull. Prince Adam's pet tiger Cringer turned into the mighty Battle Cat, He-Man's faithful companion.

Only Orko, the court magician, and Man-at-Arms, He-Man's best friend, knew this secret. Even Prince Adam's parents and Teela, captain of the guard, saw him only as the prince of Eternia. Prince Adam kept his secret because danger lived on Eternia.

On one side of the planet, the sun never shined. There, inside Snake Mountain, the wicked Skeletor planned new ways to find

out Castle Grayskull's secrets. And still others with bad intentions waited on other worlds, ready to disturb Eternia's peaceful way of life.

Against them all stood only He-Man and the Masters of the Universe!

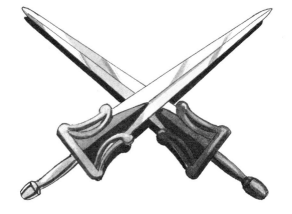

TEELA'S SECRET

Written by Bryce Knorr

Illustrated by Harry J. Quinn and James Holloway

Creative Direction by Jacquelyn A. Lloyd

Design Direction by Ralph E. Eckerstrom

A GOLDEN BOOK

Western Publishing Company, Inc.
Racine, Wisconsin 53404

Library of Congress Catalog Card Number 84-62347
ISBN 0-932631-04-5
A B C D E F G H I J

Classic™ Binding U.S. Patent #4,408,780
Patented in Canada 1984.
Patents in other countries issued or pending.
R. R. Donnelley and Sons Company

"Please, Teela," Man-at-Arms said. "Don't ask me that. I can't tell you who your mother is.

"I promised your mother on the day she gave you to me. You know what she said. 'Teela must learn who I am all by herself.'

"I can tell you only this. Your true father was one of Eternia's greatest men."

"I know you would tell me if you could, Father," Teela sighed. She walked away without seeing Prince Adam.

"Hello, Man-at-Arms," Prince Adam said. **"You and Teela both look sad. Has Teela asked you about her mother again?"**

"That's right," Man-at-Arms said. He made sure that no one else could hear them.

"You know that Sorceress is Teela's mother," Man-at-Arms said. "One day she appeared to me as Zoar and took me to her nest. There I found the baby Teela. Sorceress told me to raise Teela as my daughter. Sorceress knew it would be dangerous if anyone knew who Teela was.

"It hurts Teela not to know her mother. But someday she will learn her secret."

Teela got on Stridor and left the palace.

"I'm ready to find out who you are, Mother," Teela said. "But how? Where do I look?"

Teela rode long and hard. She stopped at a special place. Only Teela knew about the small pond ringed by tall trees.

Teela heard a woman's voice. She saw the face of a beautiful woman on the water.

"I am your mother, Teela," the woman said. But the face in the pond was not Sorceress' face. "The answer you want is at Snake Mountain. Go there."

"Snake Mountain?" Teela was surprised. The face disappeared. "But only wickedness is there."

"Teela fell for my trick," Skeletor said.
"I knew about her pond. I knew she wanted to find her mother.

"I'll help her. Teela will wear the Jewel of the Ages. She will work for me!

"First, I'll make sure He-Man is not in our way. Spikor, teach the Snow Queen a lesson. That will keep He-Man busy.

"The Snow Queen has refused to join my side. Go to her home, the Crystal Castle. Your spikes will help her get the point. Ha, ha, ha!"

Skeletor watched Teela begin her trip to Snake Mountain. He didn't see Evil-Lyn watching him. She was jealous of Teela.

"Let Teela come to Snake Mountain," Evil-Lyn said. "She won't leave there alive!"

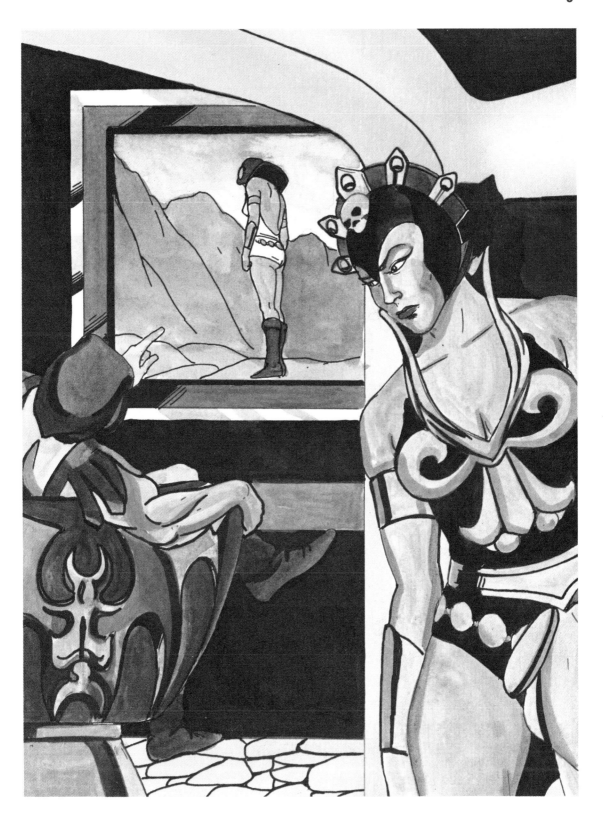

At the palace, Man-at-Arms listened to the radio. He picked up a call for help.

"It's from the Crystal Castle," he told Prince Adam. "The Snow Queen says her people are under attack!"

"He-Man will help them," Prince Adam said. **"I wish Teela could go, too. But I can't find her anywhere. I hope nothing is wrong."**

"By the power of Grayskull," Prince Adam said.

"I HAVE THE POWER!"

He-Man flew north on the fast Wind Raider. The air grew cold. The ground below turned white.

"I hope I'm not too late," He-Man said.

The Crystal Castle sparkled ahead of him. Its ice walls shone like glass in the bright sunlight.

He-Man landed. The sound of breaking ice was all around. Spikor pounded the castle.

He-Man ran up a nearby hill. He quickly packed the fluffy snow into a ball.

"He-Man is weaker than you think, Queenie," Spikor said. "He thinks he can beat me with a snowball."

He-Man didn't throw the snowball. He rolled it down the hill. The ball grew bigger and bigger. Spikor could not get out of the way.

"You are in trouble now, Spikor," He-Man said.
"Let's tell Skeletor to cool it."

He-Man loaded the snowball onto Wind Raider. When he reached Snake Mountain, Skeletor's giant snake attacked.

"Here's a present for your boss," He-Man said. He tossed the snowball on top of the snake!

As He-Man turned Wind Raider away from Snake Mountain, he saw a strange sight.

"That looked like Teela," He-Man thought. **"She went through Skeletor's gate. But it couldn't be her. Why would Teela go to Snake Mountain?"**

When Teela entered Snake Mountain, another left. Evil-Lyn went to the deepest part of the Vine Jungle.

"There it is," she said. "The portal to the Fright Zone."

A large man-eating plant opened its mouth. It swallowed Evil-Lyn whole. She traveled magically to the Fright Zone in Etheria, home of a band of wicked warriors known as The Horde. Evil-Lyn was taken prisoner when she appeared in the Fright Zone by a furry and fearsome guard.

"Who seeks Hordak?" a cold voice asked.

Grizzlor tightened his hold on Evil-Lyn.

"Tell your ugly friend to let me go, Hordak," she said. "Unless, of course, you don't want to get your hands on Skeletor."

"What do you know of him?" Hordak shouted. The Horde leader's eyes glowed with dislike.

"Let her go—for now," he commanded.

"Skeletor is right to be afraid of you," Evil-Lyn said. "But he has the Jewel of the Ages. He won't be scared for long."

"What is this Jewel?" Hordak asked.

"Whoever wears it has great power," she said. "But they must follow Skeletor's orders."

"I must have this Jewel for myself," Hordak said. "But I know you, Evil-Lyn. You want something in return. What must I give you for helping me?"

Evil-Lyn trembled with jealousy.

"Only one thing, powerful Hordak. Take the one called Teela. Make sure she never returns to Eternia!"

Teela went into Snake Mountain.

"This is a mistake," she said. "I was wrong to come here. It could be one of Skeletor's tricks."

"So you have doubts," Skeletor said. He had sneaked up on Teela from behind.

"Then look into this," Skeletor held out the Jewel of the Ages. ***"Your mother asked me to give it to you. Put it on."***

The Jewel glowed in the candlelight. As she gazed into it, Teela fell under its magic spell. She saw only the lie that Skeletor told.

"Why, it's Man-at-Arms," Teela said. "He's putting a woman in a dungeon. And stealing her baby."

"That woman is your mother," Skeletor lied. ***"And I, Skeletor, am your father."***

Teela looked into the Jewel. Skeletor's power over her grew. The longer she looked, the more she believed Skeletor's lies.

"What...do...you...want...me...to...do,...Father? she asked.

"Just this," Skeletor answered.

"Defeat Man-at-Arms! Defeat He-Man!"

Teela acted strangely when she returned to the palace. Everyone noticed it.

"She still must feel badly," Prince Adam told Man-at-Arms. **"I'll try to help her."**

"That's a pretty necklace, Teela," Prince Adam told her. **"Where did you get it?"**

"I-I don't have to tell you that," Teela answered. She left the room.

"I'm worried," Man-at-Arms said. "It's time for Teela's weapons practice. I'll talk to her."

But Teela didn't want to practice. She attacked Man-at-Arms for real. With the Jewel's power, she backed him into a corner.

Prince Adam heard Man-at-Arms' yell.

"By the power of Grayskull," Prince Adam said.

"I HAVE THE POWER!"

He-Man ran into the practice room. Teela was ready to strike Man-at-Arms. He-Man used his Power Sword to knock Teela's weapon to the floor.

"You win for now, He-Man," she said. "But Skeletor and I will beat you both!"

Teela held the Jewel. She disappeared.

"Skeletor!" Man-at-Arms cried. "How can we get Teela away from him?"

"There is only one way," He-Man said.

But when they got to Snake Mountain, they were not alone. A spaceship made of light ripped across the sky.

"Skeletor has company," He-Man said. **"That is Hordak's Light Cruiser."**

Hordak fired a ray of light at Skeletor's castle. Snake Mountain trembled and shook!

"We rang Skeletor's bell," Hordak said. "Now, we will pay him a little visit."

"Watch out for the gate," Evil-Lyn warned. "It has a trap door."

"Hordak needs no doors," the wicked leader sneered. "The Light Cruiser will take us to the heart of the mountain."

Grizzlor grabbed Evil-Lyn again.

"What should I do with the woman?" he asked.

"Bring her," Hordak said. "We'll deal with Skeletor and let her see what I have in store for her."

"You're breaking your word!" Evil-Lyn yelled. "We're supposed to be working together!"

"Here is a promise I will keep," Hordak laughed. "After we beat Skeletor, I will take care of you once and for all."

Skeletor was surprised to see Hordak.

"So, Evil-Lyn," he said.
"You are with Hordak now. It does not matter. Teela already has taken your place."

"No, Skeletor," Evil-Lyn said. "He tricked me."

"Enough talking!" Hordak yelled. He fired his ray gun. "You all must listen to me!"

"I want this Jewel of yours, Skeletor. The Jewel of the Ages, give it to me!" Hordak ordered.

"Of course," Skeletor said.

"Teela, show him the Jewel. Show him all of its power!"

Teela jumped at Hordak. Two-Bad used both his heads to fight Grizzlor and Mantenna. Leech tried to drain Skeletor's power.

Mantenna's x-ray eyes saw He-Man and Man-at-Arms outside Snake Mountain.

"He-Man is here," Mantenna told Hordak.

"Do not worry," Hordak said. "Teela will soon be mine. Then He-Man will learn the power of The Horde!"

He-Man and Man-at-Arms climbed toward Skeletor's gate.
"Be careful, He-Man," Man-at-Arms said. "Look out for traps…"
The ground under Man-at-Arms gave way.
"Hang on, Man-at-Arms!" He-man yelled. **"I'll join you."**
He jumped after his friend.

He-Man and Man-at-Arms fell down a slide. 'Round and 'round they slid.

"This probably goes straight into the mouth of one of Skeletor's pets," He-Man said.
"It's time we got off this ride."

He-Man cut a hole in the slide with his Power Sword, and he and Man-at-Arms landed in the middle of Skeletor's fight with Hordak!

"Hope you don't mind if we drop in," He-Man said. He fell on Hordak! The Horde leader went flying.

"Even The Horde cannot beat both you and Skeletor, He-Man," Hordak said. "I will be back to get you, Skeletor. You cannot escape The Horde."

Hordak and his warriors disappeared.

"*Thanks for the help, He-Man,*" Skeletor said.
"*Let me pay you back by beating you. The secrets of Castle Grayskull will be mine! Then I'll stop Hordak and rule both Eternia and Etheria!*"

"*Teela—obey the Jewel of the Ages. Attack them!*" Skeletor commanded.

Teela looked into the Jewel.

"You are my father, Skeletor. They hurt my mother. They must pay for that!"

"So that's why Teela is with Skeletor," He-Man said. **"We must get the Jewel."**

"Teela," Man-at-Arms said. "Give us the Jewel. Skeletor tricked you. He is not your father. Your mother is alive and well."

Teela stopped and looked at the Jewel. A battle raged within her between the spell of Skeletor and her loyalty to He-Man. The power of goodness was stronger than Skeletor. She took off the Jewel and gave it to He-Man.

"Here is what I think of your Jewel, Skeletor," He-Man said. He raised his Power Sword.

He-Man hit the Jewel with all his might. It blew up, and its power was gone forever.

"**Something is wrong with Teela,**" He-Man said.
"**She's fainted.**" He picked her up in his arms.

"We'd better take her right to Castle Grayskull," Man-at-Arms said. "I'm worried. Fighting Skeletor has weakened her."

"**I've had enough of Snake Mountain, too.**" He-Man said.

Skeletor was too afraid to stop them.

"Hurry, He-Man," said Sorceress' voice as they neared Castle Grayskull. "Teela needs help."

He-Man placed Teela before Sorceress. She put her hands on Teela's head.

"Wake up, my daughter," Sorceress said. "One day you will be able to call me mother."

Teela woke up. She was all right.

"I wanted to know my mother so much I even believed Skeletor's lies," Teela said.

"Sometimes," Sorceress said. "We can want things too much. When we want things very much, we may do things that aren't very smart. And that can be unkind, or even dangerous, to ourselves and our friends."

"But I would like to know who my mother is," Teela said. "I want her to be proud of me."

Sorceress kept her secret.

"Someday you will know, Teela," Sorceress told her. "It is something you must find out on your own.

"But this I know for sure. Your mother is very, very proud of you and your courage."

THE END